SUPER
ROOTABILITIES

the Rootlets

SUPER ROOTABILITIES

Written by Vicki Marquez   Illustrated by Jeremy Russnak

To my love and my life partner, Saul… you are my Super Rootability and without you this book would be only a dream. Thank you for lifting me higher than I ever thought I could go.

There are a few other incredible people who have helped me turn this dream into a reality: Jeremy Russnak, my insanely talented and one-of-a-kind illustrator, who took a vision from my imagination and made it real, and Julie Knight, my word wizard and brilliantly wonderful editor, who taught me true alchemy using the beautiful magic of good literature. Thank you also to Taryn Dufault for taking all of the pieces and tying them together.

Up in the solar system, many moons away from Planet Earth, hangs a small and enchanted planet called Planet Planted. The people who live in this magical plant-based world all grew from the ground, like a beautiful garden.

The Rootlets – Brocc, Carrotina, Cornelius and Kaley – live in Planet Planted's VeggieVille with their dog, Basil, and Yammy Grammy, their guardian and caretaker, who picked them from the ground when they were just tiny little sprouts. In VeggieVille, everyone has colorful vegetable hair, but only the Rootlets have magical powers called Rootabilities. With the help of Yammy Grammy and her best friend, Mr. Fungo Fungi, these four little Rootlets are on a journey of self-discovery, adventure and unexpected surprise.

When the Rootlets awoke on a regular autumn day, it took just a moment before Brocc realized that it was anything BUT regular.

Today would be big...**bigger than big**...**bigger than a thousand-pound pumpkin big!**

"Get up, everybody!" he shouted to his friends, shaking the bright green florets that sprung from his head. "Today's Earthrise! Our once-in-a-lifetime chance to see Planet Earth!"

"I've waited my whole life for this day and it's finally here!" he exclaimed to Carrotina, Kaley and Cornelius, who rubbed their eyes and smiled at their friend's excitement.

Then he carefully picked up his prized Onion SkySearcher XT8 telescope, fine-tuned the lens and gently set it back on his desk.

He could barely contain his excitement as he thought about viewing Planet Earth and sketching his observations for the next cover of *National Plantographic* magazine!

Before the Rootlets could respond, there was a knock at the door, and from the funny-sounding pattern – *tap-tap-tap, pause, tap-tap, pause, tap* – they knew exactly who it was: Mr. Fungo Fungi.

Mr. Fungi was Yammy Grammy's best friend, and every time he came for a visit he announced his arrival the same way: "Fungo here, Fungi there, fun-go fun-gi everywhere!"

Mr. Fungi had a funny way of talking in circles, which often confused people, and he believed in magical things, like legends and folk tales. When people first met him, they weren't sure what to think, but Yammy would always say: "Give Mr. Fungi time and he'll grow on you."

The Rootlets loved Mr. Fungi because he was… a fun guy! He owned Plantasy Land – the largest, most brilliant, most magnificent (and only!) amusement park, and he always made the Rootlets laugh with his crazy stories and odd way of speaking. It was great fun when Mr. Fungi was around!

But today was different. Today, Yammy said that the grown-ups needed to talk... *privately*.

Even Basil wasn't allowed to sit with the grown-ups.

This made the Rootlets very nervous, so they did what any curious kids would do: they pressed their ears against the sweet potato brick wall and listened carefully. Mr. Fungi sounded worried and talked very fast. He spoke of a special legend book that said that on the eighth day of the eleventh month, when Planet Earth would appear, those with the letter "R" on the heel of their foot would learn of their super magical powers – called *Rootabilities!*

"Sounds like some lucky duck is becoming a superhero today," said Kaley. "I wonder why Yammy didn't want us to hear that?"

Carrotina nervously lifted her foot and showed her friends.

"I have an 'R'," she whispered. "I saw it yesterday, when I was doing yoga. Maybe Mr. Fungi is talking about me."

"Woo hoo!" exclaimed Cornelius, pulling off his sock.

"I have one, too – look! *I'm a superhero with my super powers. I will climb up towers with my super powers,*" he sang as he twirled his sock over his head.

"Goody goody gumdrops, so do I!" said Kaley happily as she peeked at her foot. "Maybe mine stands for rhinestones?"

"I also have one," added Brocc, examining his foot.

"That means we ALL have super Rootabilites and it sounds like we need to discover them before Earthrise tonight!"

The Rootlets returned their ears to the wall and listened as Mr. Fungi explained in his confusing way of speaking.

"Either these powers are powers that they know about already – which I presume they don't – or they are powers that they DO NOT yet know about – which I presume they do. If the latter is true, then this is a BIG day for our little Rootlets!"

Yammy poured a glass of warm green tea and held up an old, dusty legend book.

"Read it, Fungo, please," she said.

Mr. Fungi carefully turned the pages of the book until he found the page marked with an X. He cleared his throat and began:

"Legend foretells that an R on the heel shall one day reveal: all that's heavy, be light, in darkness, shine bright, what's far shall be near, the unknown, crystal clear. To help the one that is stronger than these, four must master their Rootabilities."

"So then it IS true?" asked Mr. Fungi, half nervously, half excitedly.

Yammy looked up with a twinkle in her eye.

"Yes, Fungo, it's true."

thought Yammy said that we're special, because everybody's special," whispered Kaley. "I didn't know that she meant we were extra special, with magic abilities and crystal wands."

"Who said anything about crystal wands?" asked Cornelius.

"If I have super powers," replied Kaley, "I'll definitely need a crystal wand. What's a power without pizazz?"

"Well," said Brocc, "let's get started! We'll use the clues from the legend book to help us figure it out. But we have to work fast. Discovering our Rootablilities won't be easy and we need to finish by sundown so that we don't miss Earthrise!"

"I'm invisible, that's my Rootability!" said Cornelius, placing his hands over his eyes.

"Nobody can see me!"

"YES WE CAN!" giggled the group.

.ROOTABILITIES.

The Legend

Legend Foretells.....

An "R" on the heel
Shall one day reveal
All that is heavy,be light
In darkness, shine bright
What's far shall be near
The unknown, crystal clear
To help the one that is stronger than these
Four must master their Rootabilities

The Rootlets each grabbed their favorite green power juice box for energy and then piled around the table to solve the biggest mystery of their lives.

They started by reading up on all sorts of powers – from wizards to witches, magicians to superheroes – then tested them all to see what would happen. But the spells wouldn't cast, the broomsticks wouldn't fly, the hats wouldn't make rabbits appear and the capes wouldn't carry them up through the air. Nothing worked. Minutes turned to hours as the Rootlets puzzled over their mysterious Rootabilites.

Mr. Fungi called out, "So long, Rootlet Littles!" as
Yammy peeked her head in the room.
"What are you up to in here?" she asked.

"We're busy working on a mystery," said Carrotina.

"Well, how about some dinner?" asked Yammy. "It's almost sundown!"

Their tummies growled and the Rootlets agreed that Yammy's yummy roasted root vegetable soup was just what they needed to fuel up before getting back to work.

After dinner, Cornelius was bursting with energy and ready to prove that invisibility was most certainly his Rootability. He squeezed his eyes shut, then began walking around the room, first bumping into the bed, then the wall, then headed straight toward Brocc's desk.

"Can you see me now?" he asked.

"Yes, but, LOOK OUT!" yelled Brocc, but it was too late.

Cornelius walked right into Brocc's desk, and with a loud thump, slam, bang and crash, the desk shattered into a thousand pieces. The Rootlets stood frozen in shock, staring at the pile of rubble and Brocc's beloved SkySearcher, now just a twisted piece of metal and broken glass.

"Cornelius, you broke Brocc's desk!" whispered Carrotina.

"NO, NO, NO!" Brocc uttered in disbelief. "Nevermind the desk, he broke my telescope! Now I won't be able to see Earth – and if I can't see it, I can't draw it! I'm doomed!"

"I'm SO sorry Brocc, I didn't mean to," Cornelius apologized.

Yammy rushed into the room. "What was that loud noise?" she asked.

"We were trying to figure out our super Rootabilities, when Cornelius accidentally banged into Brocc's desk and broke his telescope," explained Kaley.

"Your super Rootabilites? How did you know about that?" Yammy asked, raising an eyebrow.

"We accidently, well, on purpose, overheard Mr. Fungi telling you about them," Brocc admitted as a single tear rolled down his cheek.

At that very moment, Carrotina looked out the window and shrieked, **"Holy moly – it's beautiful!"**

"What is?" asked Cornelius.

"The Earth. It's HUGE. Can't you guys see it?"

"No!" sputtered Brocc. "We don't have the telescope, remember?"

"Well, I don't have a telescope either, but I..." Carrotina began.

Brocc interrupted. "You can see it, without the telescope? Then that's your Rootability! It's like the riddle said – *what's far shall be near* – you can see faraway things! Quick! What else can you see? Maybe I can still draw it after all!"

Carrotina focused on Earth, rattling off observations that Brocc would never have been able to see – even with his super spectacular telescope.

"There are shiny buildings and roads and mountains... and...and...people! With funny stuff on their heads...I think...it could be...hair? Yes, definitely hair!"

Brocc quickly sketched every detail, drawing a picture perfect Planet Earth, complete with people...who have hair!

"I'm sorry Brocc, I can't look anymore," said Carrotina, sadly. "My eyes hurt!"

"It's too much, too soon. Your Rootablilites are only newly sprouting," explained Yammy. "You're going to have to learn how and when to use these powers – otherwise they can be very dangerous. Let's shut off the lights and give your eyes a rest."

Cornelius switched off the light and Carrotina closed her eyes in the darkness. But moments later, it was as if the lights had gone on again – full blast!

Carrotina opened her eyes and quickly looked around the room. "Kaley! You're glowing!" she squealed. "Your skin is sparkling like diamonds!"

"Oh, YAY!" shouted Kaley. "I LOVE diamonds! This is so much better than having a crystal wand!" she said, spinning around the room, glowing brighter and brighter.

"Wait, the riddle," Brocc reminded the group. "*In darkness, shine bright.* As soon as we turned off the lights, Kaley began to shine. That must be your Rootability!"

Cornelius turned to Yammy.

"What about Brocc and me?" he asked sadly. "What are our Rootabilities?"

"Brocc knows," she replied with a grin.

"Cornelius, I've got it!" Brocc revealed. "Didn't you find it strange that a small guy such as yourself could have so much power to demolish an entire desk and everything on it, just by bumping into it?"

"I guess I didn't think about that," replied Cornelius. "So I AM invisible?"

"No, silly, your Rootablity is strength," replied Brocc. "*All that's heavy, be light.* You are very, very strong! So things that are heavy will seem light to you."

"AWESOME!" Cornelius said proudly, flexing his teeny tiny muscles. "What about you, Brocc? What's your Rootability?"

"Well, I figured out the entire riddle," replied Brocc. "*Making the unknown crystal clear*, so maybe my Rootability is super brainpower! Is that right, Yammy?"

Yammy smiled proudly.

"Yes, Brocc, you're right," she said. "You each have your very own super Rootabilities, and that makes you uniquely special: Carrotina, your super vision; Kaley, your super skin; Cornelius, your super strength; and Brocc, your super intelligence. Now that you know what your Rootabilites are, it's my job to help you learn how to use them, and always for good. And it's YOUR job to develop them with care."

"Let's start now!" shrieked Kaley. "I want to go light up the night!"

Brocc hopped up and grabbed his books.

"I'm heading to the library," he said. "I've got a report to write on Planet Earth."

Carrotina grabbed a sweater and headed for the door.

"I'm going to climb the big oak tree in the yard and gaze at the nighttime sky," she said. "I'll bet I can count a thousand different stars!"

"And I'm feeling extra strong," exclaimed Cornelius. "Would you like me to rearrange the living room furniture, Yammy?"

"Hold on, my dears!" said Yammy with a chuckle. "I know you're all anxious to test out your special gifts, and there's plenty of time for that. But right now, it's time for bed. If you want to become Planet Planted's own special superheroes, it's best to start after a good night's sleep."

Brocc dropped his books and stretched.

"You're right, Yammy," he said with a yawn. "I have a feeling we're going to need all the rest we can get."

And with that, all four Rootlets climbed into their beds and under the covers, as Yammy whispered, "Sweet dreams. Tomorrow's adventure is just a few hours away…"

THE END

Explore the magical world of Planet Planted and follow The Rootlets on their many adventures!

JOIN THE FAN CLUB!
WWW.THEROOTLETS.COM

And be sure to follow along on

About the Author:

In *The Rootlets: Super Rootabilities,* Vicki Marquez introduces readers to Brocc, Carrotina, Cornelius and Kaley – four fun-loving and adventurous kids with veggie hair and healthy habits.

As a certified health coach, wellness expert, plant-based chef and author, Vicki's dream is to break the stigma that healthy living is boring and to show both kids and adults that plants – especially veggies – are ridiculously cool!

Vicki lives in Chicago, with her husband, stepdaughter and two quinoa-loving Yorkies.

About the Illustrator:

Jeremy Russnak is an illustrator from Chicago. He has created illustrations for *Time Out* magazine, the *Chicago Reader* and other publications. He is currently residing in Los Angeles pursuing his passion in the field of animation.